Amelia,
you make me happy.
I love you.
xxx

The Adventures of Oreo, Domino and Chess

a story by Rani

In a cosy little Cheshire cottage, there lives three black and white cats. Oreo is the mother cat, and Chess and Domino are her two daughters. They are the happiest cats around, always exploring and making new friends.

One sunny morning, Oreo decided it was time for an adventure. The three cats set out together and as they walked along they saw tall trees with colourful leaves, sparkling streams, and fields full of flowers. They smelled the fresh air and felt the warmth of the sun on their fur.

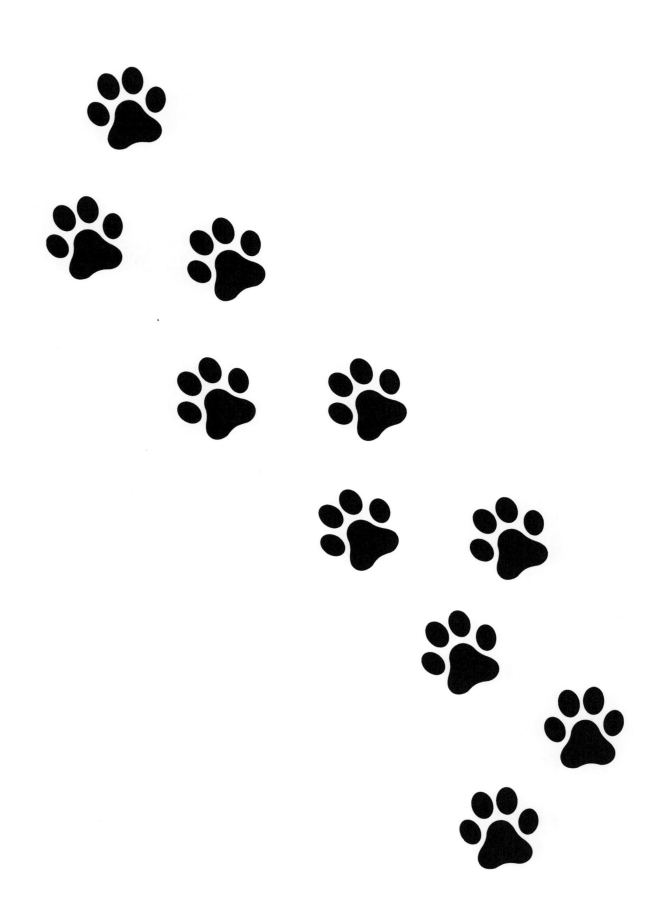

As they walked, they met a friendly dog named Tia, who showed them how to dig holes in the dirt before teaching her three fury friends how to clean the dirt from their paws and claws.

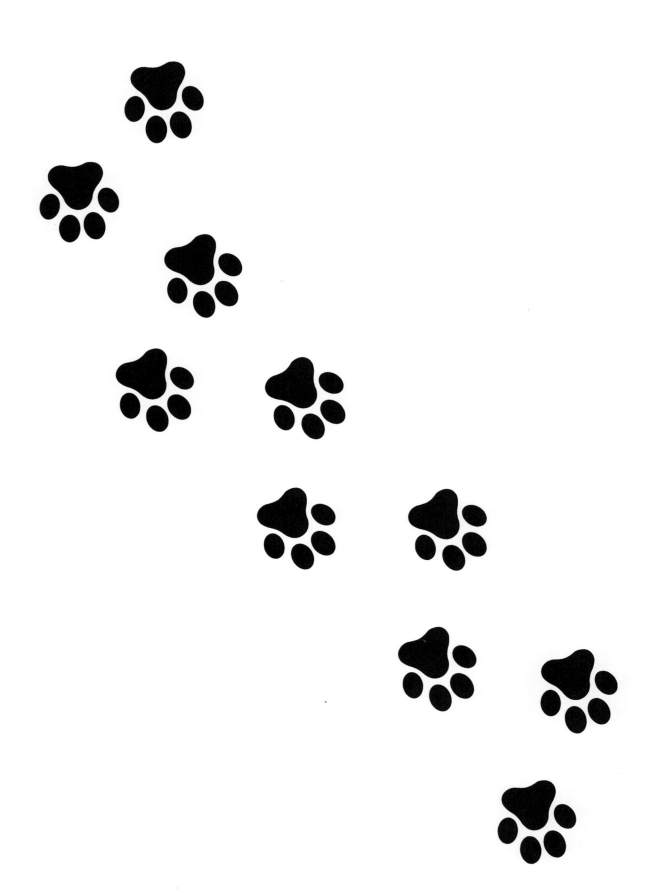

As they continued exploring they came across a tall tree with a low hanging branch.

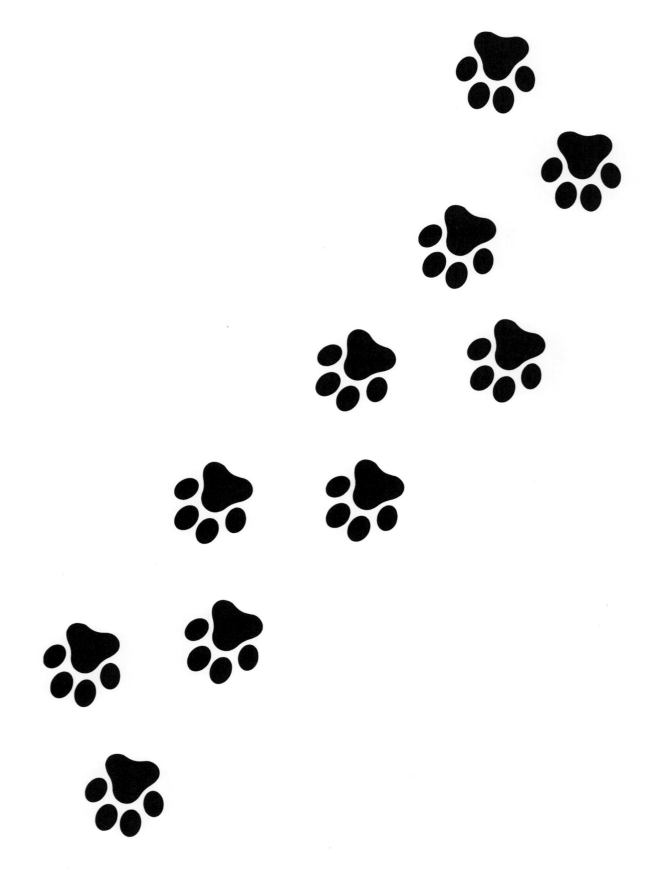

Chess was feeling playful and she was the first to try and climb it, but she fell down! She was not hurt, but she was too scared to try again.

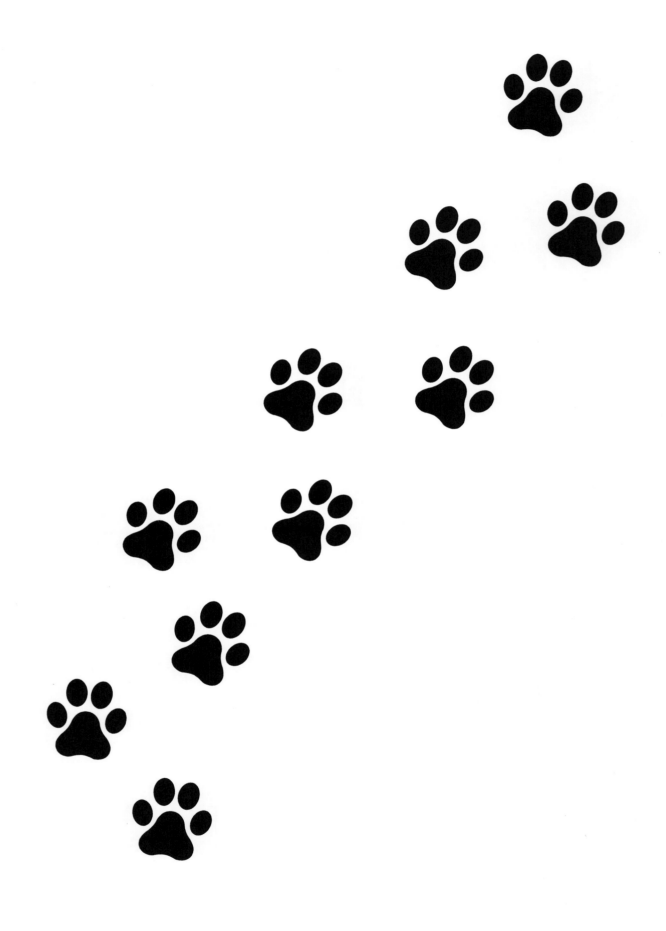

Domino tried next, but she was too afraid of heights and did not make it very far!

Oreo knew that she had to do
something to help Domino and Chess
overcome their fears.

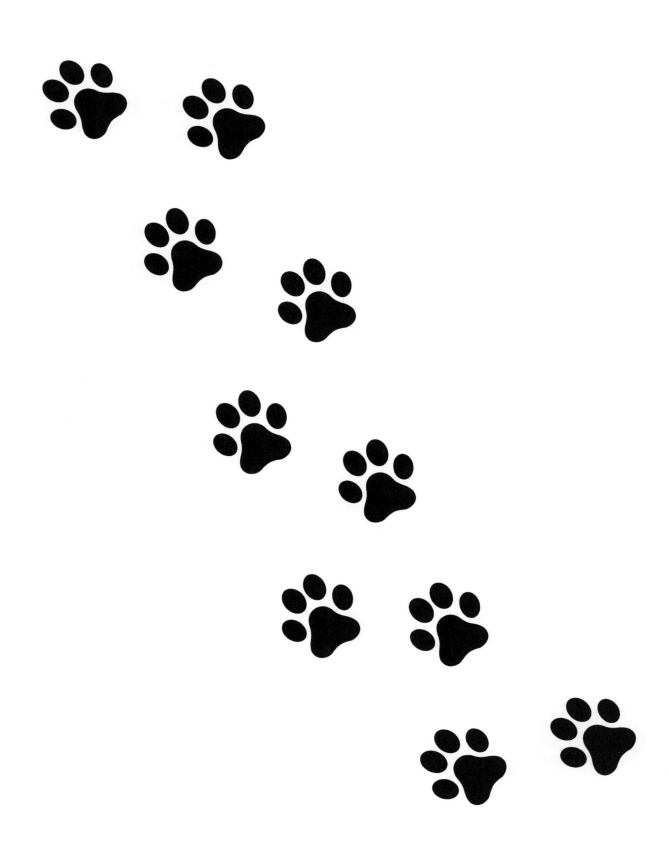

Oreo climbed up the tree and meowed down to Domino and Chess. "Come on, girls"! she meowed loudly. "You can do it. Just take it one step at a time."

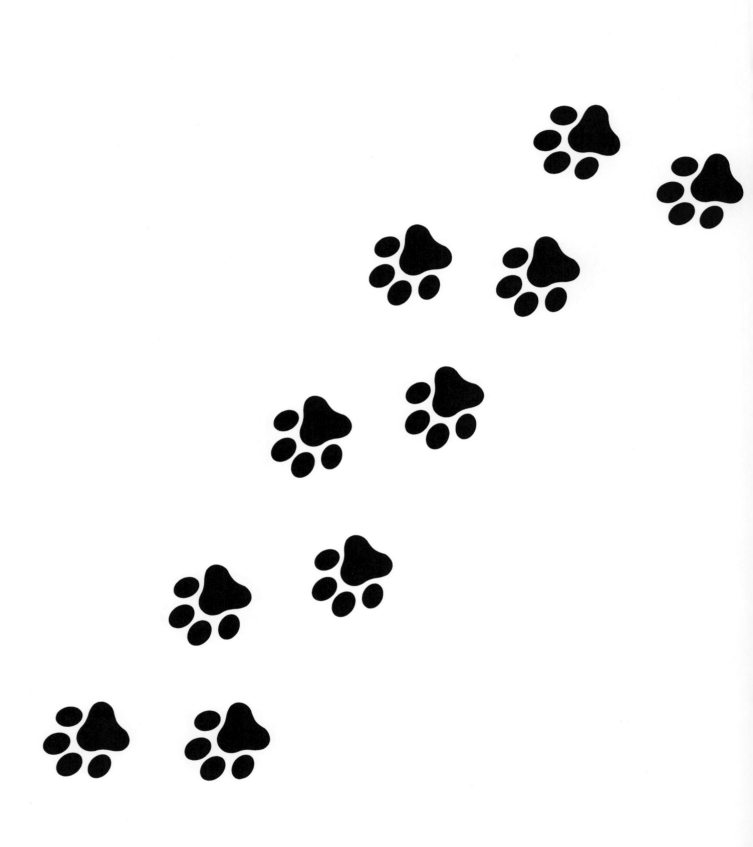

Chess and Domino watched as Oreo climbed higher and higher. Oreo's encouragement helped Chess and Domino to try again.

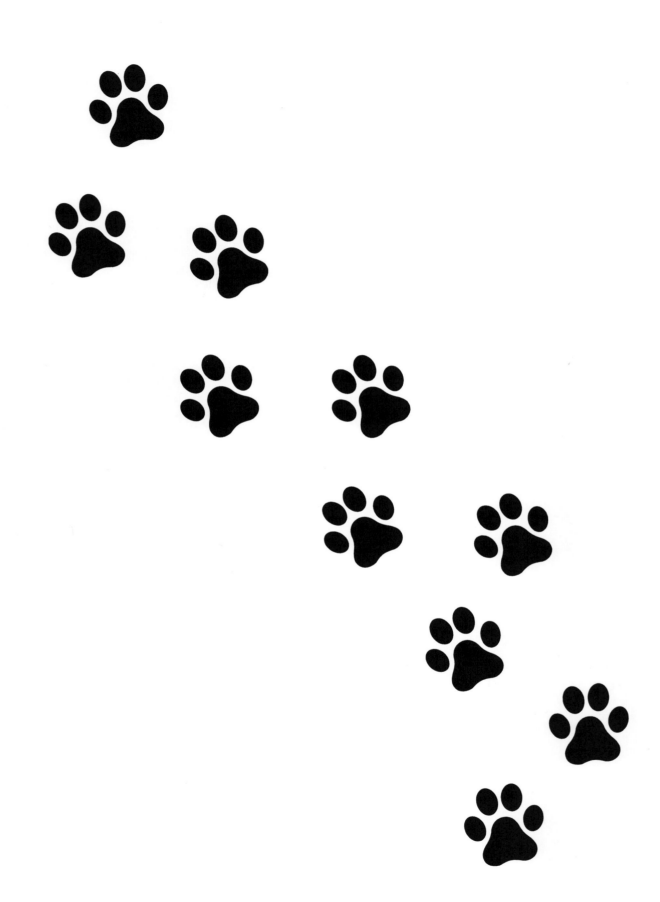

This time, paw step after paw step they made it to the top of the tree! With all the noise of climbing the tree the cats woke up a sleeping resident.

They had woken a wise old owl named Hootie, who told them all sorts of stories about the world.

Hootie seemed to know so much about what goes on in the Cheshire countryside, and he definitely knew who's who. Hoo's hoo.

After such a busy day they returned
to their cosy cottage, tired but
content. They curled up together
purring, fell asleep and dreamt of
their next big adventure.

till next time...

Printed in Great Britain
by Amazon

26281589R00021